Tabish Nawaz takes readers through a fascinating journey through the nebulous landscapes of lived experience, dreams and imagery, as all the while running beneath the surface, the strands of cultural memory and deep political understanding merge seamlessly.

GAUTAM BENEGAL

Tabish Nawaz

Opening Clouds Fermented Rain

Tabish Nawaz

HAWAKAL

CALCUTTA | NEW DELHI

hawakal

CALCUTTA | NEW DELHI

Hawakal Publishers

33/1/2 K B Sarani, Mall Road, Calcutta 80
70-B/9 Amritpuri, East of Kailash, New Delhi 65

Email info@hawakal.com
Website www.hawakal.com

First edition August, 2020

Cover photograph: Hera Iqbal
Cover design: Bitan Chakraborty

ISBN: 978-81-946651-1-3

Price: 300 INR | USD 13.99

for
Papa, Ammi,
and the City of New Bedford

ACKNOWLEDGMENTS

Papa inspired me to read good literature and as widely as possible. Papa, who not only brought me books but also used to ask me to provide him a summary of what I had last read. This was a conscious effort on his part to initiate me to not only read and enjoy but also to communicate my understanding. Ammi, herself an avid reader, inspired me by making me curious as to what she always read in Urdu. Ladwi Mama for living inside a book-house virtually, whereby merely standing, as a child, I used to feel reverence for books. My teachers at Oak Grove School, notable among them Mr. Bhatt, Mr. Anand Kumar, Mr. Raza, Mr. Rajiv Kishore, Late Dr. Naqvi, Dr. Dubey, Mr. Shariq, Mr. Raturi, Mr. Shee and Mr. Vinay Kumar who nurtured me as a family and guided me to read and write well.

My lifelong friends and seniors from OG—particularly Mrityunjay, Nikhil, Satish, Shitanshu, Puneet Sir, Kanishka Sir, Pragati Ma'am—they have been reading my mad mumblings over the years. Their encouragement has kept me going over the years.

My friends from IIT Kharagpur: Abhishek Ranjan 'Cobra,' Gaurav Anurag, Anubhav Pratap Singh 'Doga,' Rahul 'Lucky Guy,' and Tiwariji—their numerous 'bhaat' sessions at Tikka, Chedi, and behind Meta department. These mindless chit-chats (bhaat) gave me multiple ways of looking at the world.

My friends at STF, Reliance in Jamnagar: Pankaj, Arun, Anurodh, Himanshu, Gaurav, Ashish, Sanjay Sir, Vibhor, among many—they ignited in me the passion for writing fiction and poetry and who were among the first to see and appreciate.

Special mention to my mentor and advisor, Dr. Sukalyan Sengupta, whose guidance and the discussion helped me to broaden my mental horizon to engage with philosophy, poetry, and literature beyond my scientific discipline.

Last but not least, my siblings and family: Faizi, Bhabhi, Shuby, Jawed Bhai, Boy Ma, Bunty, Imran Bhai, Rana, Nazish, Saba, Arish, Nabeel, Munne, Munnin, Arqu, Saru and Bismu for finding worth in my writing even when I doubted it. Without their support, I would have never even thought about this book.

Special mention to my better half, Hera, who bore my reading and writing activities with patience, understood, with grace, my need for them. Time, I dedicate for reading and writing is also the time I make myself unavailable to her. Without Hera's support, this journey would have been impossible.

Many thanks to my publishers: *Indian Review*, *eFiction India*, *Flash Fiction Magazine*, *Temper Literary Review*, *Oakgrovians*, *The Punch Magazine*, and *Ethos Literary Journal* for first publishing some of the stories in this collection.

Hearty gratitude to Kiritida for giving me this fantastic opportunity, without whose timely intervention, the book would not have materialized. Also, thanks to Mr. Bitan Chakraborty and *Hawakal Publishers* for publishing this work and bringing it out to a broader audience. I hope *Opening Clouds, Fermented Rain* would bring hope, smile, and empathy to my readers.

Tabish Nawaz
July 17, 2020
IIT Bombay Campus,
India

Contents

CARPET BOMBING

When I first heard the word 'carpet bombing,' I was a kid then, an eighth-grader, to be precise. I knew carpet; we had one. Mother brought it with her, in dowry, and often looking at it, she used to sigh about her good old days. It used to hang on the wall of our living room, where guests used to come and sit. Whenever I used to see it sun drying and later, dust being beaten out of it, I instantly used to know that a guest visit was imminent. It used to be kept near the sofa where guests used to sit and put their feet on. It caused softness to their feet and conveyed a false impression of our well-being, and in a sense, of opulence.

After the guests had left, the mother would delicately clean it with her hands, meticulously picking up the food crumbs and then leaving it to dry in the sunlight. The only thing we had in plenty in our home that was otherwise a shanty, beyond the living room. And the guests never ventured ahead.

The carpet, therefore, enjoyed an elevated status in our home. It preserved our ancestral prosperity—at least in the eyes of our guests and hid the potholes poverty had made in our lives.

Therefore, this word 'carpet bombing' piqued my curiosity. I searched for its meaning in an old, worn-out dictionary, which I think belonged to the Jurassic era when the world was unaware of anything existing by that name. Internet was too wary of entering our neighborhood, whose majority of dwellers knew only to forage during the day and sleep in the night.

'Carpet bombing,' therefore, loitered in my consciousness only for a few days, and then life ran over it and settled it like a roadkill which cakes after repeated running over by vehicles and dries by sunlight and helplessly becomes part of the road and dissolves into the landscape.

The path of my life was paved with many such flattened questions, which in turn burdened and flattened life itself.

After the tenth grade, my studies got over. My father was growing old, and so was his capability to feed the family. In my neighborhood, it was the natural course every educational pursuit took. However, it used to start with much hope and sacrifices.

The sight of kids going to school gave every elder a break from their harried lives. It was a much-needed make-believe system to live through an otherwise unbearable daily life of maddening physical labor and meager income. They would collect all their dreams in the school bags of their children—the bags which they could afford only once in their lives, and whom poverty, with its sharp fangs, used to riddle with holes, through which all their dreams would trickle, slip and eventually transmogrify into their lives, which were lived by their children and then their children, with just as much hope as their children.

Countless lives, so repetitive, so familiar to all, as if without beginning or end, just like reality, always present and never for a moment going out of focus. Even in their nightly dreams, they dreamt of life. Daily life—saturated, massive, present, widespread, and lived identically by all its inhabitants.

Therefore, escaping the life of the neighborhood was not easy. Even their dreams failed to do that. And then the war happened in our neighboring country.

The war was business not only for gods of the earth but also for tiny, faceless earthlings like us. First, a country was destroyed, and then it was rebuilt. It was the highest profit-making business idea of my age. Though in such a period, economic benefits justified almost anything, yet it was an ancient norm to initiate the war in the name of nation, freedom, and democracy. Embellishing was such a human trait then.

The war in the neighborhood coincided with the drying up of my country's economy. Later, I heard that it was not a mere coincidence; it had always happened like that. This ploy made sure that ordinary people, in whose name wars were fought, engaged in wars out of economic reasons. Experience suggested that nationalism, freedom, democracy, and demonization of "the other" were necessary but not sufficiently equipped to sustain a long-term war. Yet strangely, economic reasons alone used to put closure on any conflict, but not without citing the lofty ideals of human rights and peace. Again, embellishing was very social.

In such a deprived atmosphere, appeared one day a job contractor, looking for young men, for jobs in the war-torn nation. He caused a significant upheaval in the neighborhood. People began to hide their actual ages from one another. However, it was not much of a trouble since many of its dwellers were not even aware of their actual birthdays, forget precise birth dates. But people recollected major events, even minor ones, of their lives by mentioning the movies they saw that time, their release date acted as their timeline, their calendar.

"You remember my marriage?"—inquired one.

And, if the other found it hard to recollect.

"*Sholay* was in the theatre."—used to come to the cue.

"Yes, yes, I remember," and with this, the recipient of this newly found memory would bring forth even the minor details: "I danced on that song, and I wore the jacket like Jai and had my hair combed like Viru." All his descriptions related to the movie, as if the marriage happened only to celebrate the film.

In a sense, it was, since people used to plan major events of their lives only when some hit movie was playing out in the theatre. Maybe it brought a sense of time in their otherwise timeless lives, a feeling of change in their otherwise constant daily lives, and a notion of keeping memories in lives that knew only the present. This artifice gave them a means to look beyond their present, which was perpetual and pervasive since their woes never saw an ending. Generation after generation, the struggle to survive remained as similar as ever, giving them an understanding that time is unchangeable and endless. They could never make out the boundaries of time that separate its three constituents. Therefore, movies at least gave them a vague sense that something happened in life that was different from their normal daily lives, and their recollections cheered them.

Therefore, the arrival of the job contractor made old movies and songs a pariah. People, mostly middle-aged ones, feigned ignorance about them or their release. And if someone accidentally hummed them or mentioned them, then a display of youthful exuberance used to follow, often in the form of affected public brawls or mindless swearing.

People began to appear clean-shaven all the time—faces scrubbed with anything that produced lather, some even with the soil. Some dyed their hair with stolen *Henna* leaves, collected from the public park. People who were past their prime were often seen in garishly colorful shirts and trousers.

In their attempt to appear juvenile, they publicly hurled lewd remarks to the passing girls. At other times, these would have been done furtively, and nobody would have even noticed. But in those days, that was the whole purpose. To the delight of every male participant, including the relatives of the aggrieved, the tiff was vigorously pursued, and masculine energy was overtly displayed. Since more than honor, about which the dwellers had the least idea, livelihood was at stake. A reason purely economic, but never stated. Economics, much like the Baudelaire's devil, tricked everyone about its non-existence, while running almost every human affair nonetheless.

Soon my neighborhood was gripped with a strange fever with juvenility as its symptom but a profound and mature urge for economic survival as its cause. It even touched the juvenile population. And it added a previously unknown facet to the juvenility where people *acted* their age, not under any hormonal or physical changes but more out of the economic competition. They looked as absurd as their grown-up counterparts. Juvenility, thus, lost its natural course everywhere, becoming a simulated exam, which everyone intended to pass without making any mistakes. But what is there to juvenility without its thoughtlessness and its related mistakes?

Affected acts, however big or small, need dissemination. Therefore, amid a quiet economic environment, the only business that flourished was of tea stalls. These little tea shops, usually housed in cabins along the roadside, appeared at a feverish pace in my neighborhood, became part of the landscape, and in a short time, usurped it.

These mainly functioned as a gathering point for people where daily affairs were talked about, blown out of proportion, and spread. In such a time where intentional acts supposedly needed to reach every corner of the neighborhood, these became indispensable. More than selling tea and low-quality moistened snacks; they served to market news and rumors, mostly the latter. To add more to their usefulness, these tea shops named themselves accordingly—Newspoint Tea Shop, News Center Tea Shop, Newsmakers Tea Stall, Newswallah, etc.

These shops bustled with an odd consortium of people belonging to middle, old and young ages, sitting and chatting together. Some willingly and some unwillingly dissolved the barriers of time and age that separated them. The middle-aged ones, due to their precarious position, used to be the most vocal and giggling and often took umbrage at the slightest of allusion about their fakeness. They were the ones who came to blows quite quickly.

Tea sellers would take much delight in such brawls, often announcing free tea and snacks for the winners of such fisticuffs. Some even started selling the tea in the name of the winner of the day, creating awareness of brands in the minds of the uneducated, naïve dwellers.

Later, when these winners turned up at the job contractor's for an interview, they cited the eponymous teas in these tea shops, as a certificate of their strength, exuberance, and energy. This mass-show of juvenility did work out for some, but for most, it drove them in a state of perpetual juvenility. I presume similar things happened elsewhere too.

I, too, applied for the job. Not only because I needed it, but also because I was an also-ran. Being also-ran was not what I wanted, but it was familiar and safer.

It rained for an hour on the night before my interview. But the roof of our house rained for another four hours. The mother had meticulously ironed my last school uniform for the meeting. It had a tie too. I last wore it two years back at a wedding. It was the only decent dress I had.

Though it rained, the mother carefully wrapped the dress in a polythene bag and tucked it under her pillow and slept over it. In the morning, she was wet, but she did not allow a drop in my interview dress. Perhaps it was the only thing that remained dry that morning. It made me sad and brought tears to my eyes, which later spilled over my dress, making it wet, and thus, sanctifying it.

I reached the job center two hours before the scheduled time. But there were other people—a lot of them had been sleeping outside the gate since the night before. My school dress, which had become shorter at my ankles and wrists, as most of my dresses were, became an object of ridicule and amusement.

"Look, he is trying to fake his age by wearing the school dress."—said some middle-aged ones.

"Uncle, the school is that way."—mocked the youths.

Though it had been only three years since I dropped out of school after the tenth grade, I looked much older than my actual age. It was not my emaciated body that betrayed my age but my face, which looked faded, decolorized, and worried most of the time.

I exhibited a flustered smile at these gibes.

Had there been someone else at my place, an exchange of words must have ensued. I shared the neighborhood and its poverty, yet we were not one of them in many ways, we had seen our days of prosperity, and awareness of it filled our behavior with grace and prevented us from any confrontation with them, but not without labeling us, among our neighbors, with a tag of pretentious vanity.

Overcoming the public stare and ridicule, I reached the registration desk. The receptionist was a middle-aged man. He was holding a plastic toothpick whose pointed end was occasionally moving between his teeth and sometimes scratching his back and neck. He had an old newspaper on his desk, from which he never raised his head and eyes. He was a man of few words. He did not bother to look at me when I reached the desk.

He only asked, "Age?"—in a voice that almost choked with death.

"Twenty-two."—the response came out.

Then the toothpick pointed to his left and moved back and forth. I obliged and joined a sea of people, some young and some middle-aged ones, but all of them supposedly under twenty-two.

"They are very particular about the age. I have seen people being thrown out for faking their age."—said a man, who visibly had hair only in his nose. I was standing next to him. To avoid further discussion, I feigned indifference and tried to move away from him. He sensed my lack of interest, yet he tried to minimize the gap that existed between us.

"I have been coming here almost daily. I know what is happening. They say there are things one can never hide after an age." He added to involve me in the conversation.

By staring long at him and listening to his words, I realized that one thing one can never hide after a certain age is age. Despite removing all his hairs, his age was peeping from his nose, in the form of whitened hairs, which he often tried to hide while talking, by inserting his fingers and pulling them out. But the more he pulled out or shoved inside, the more they appeared as if that little nose had housed a whole grapevine of hair inside it. And, the more he looked aged.

The gap that he wished to minimize appeared less of a physical one now. He was only making himself comfortable in an age group to which he never really belonged. Maybe he was trying to melt away and be homogenous with the crowd so that he was not picked up by the prying eyes and thrown away. The idea of an onlooker observing us made me move away from him.

A bell sounded. A round man holding a register appeared. He was wearing a faded cotton vest. Hairs from his armpit were furiously creeping outside, mottled and like bristles. His approach towards me made the other man move behind my back.

"He's the one."—I heard him murmuring from behind.

He stood in front of me. His hand moved slightly on the register. The movement parted his arms from his body and revealed his armpit, relaxing the shrub that grew there. It released a long-suppressed stench that almost made me unconscious.

"Age?"—he asked gruffly.

"Twenty-two."

He looked me in my eyes, held it there for a while. Then his probing eyes gradually descended, resting partially at my chest and genital, finally focusing on his register.

"Forty-six"—he shouted.

"What?"—I asked.

He shoved me to his right, the stench that emanated from his armpits followed me for a while. I stumbled for a few steps before gaining my gait. To this day, I am uncertain that what made me stumble more that day—his shove or his stench?

Even today, remembering that moment fills me with nausea. I was then taken to a room, where a man with the doctor's gear was sitting, reading a cheap, worn-out comic, named *Doga ko Gado* (Bury Doga).

"Number forty-six?"

"Yesss."

Before I finished saying 'yes,' I was put on a weighing machine. He then measured my height, heartbeat, blood pressure, noted them down on a piece of paper, and handed it back to me. With a movement of his hand, he asked me to go through a door located on his left. He then got busy with his comic, smilingly.

At that door, a smiling man greeted me.

"Congratulations!"

"Oh! Thanks!"

Without bothering for my reply, he held out his hand towards me. I mistakenly thought it to be a customary handshake and offered my hand in response. He then groped for my thumb and pressed them on an ink pad and later on several forms, which were strewn all over the table. With the continuing motion, he pushed me to the wall and took a few of my photographs.

"Deposit the money for your travel and visa."

The thing about money worried me.

"I don't have money to pay."

"No problem. Put your thumb here."—He said, pulling out another form.

"I can sign. I know that."

"We don't keep pens. You put it here." He took my thumb and stamped the form.

"Listen, you will not be paid for the first three months. You will be provided with food and accommodation, though. Your salary will go towards paying for your travel expenses."

"Now leave. You are done. Be here tomorrow at 9 in the morning with your clothes and belongings."

I was led out through the back door.

On my way home, I stopped at the tea shop. Many people, including tea sellers, gathered around me. They asked me about my selection, and on hearing that I did, they offered me tea and gloated how regularly I had tea at their shops those days. They also made a note of my name and address. And, before I left, they stuffed my pocket with moistened snacks, which I munched to my home.

The news of my selection reached home before me. The mother was at the gate, waiting for me eagerly. I could see her from a distance. On seeing her, my steps gathered pace, as if pulled in by some mysterious force. It had been years since I last saw my mother smiling. The smile on her face emanated light and brought brilliance to the faded landscape.

At the doorsteps, she hugged me and caressed my forehead. Tears began to well up in her eyes, which added luster to her smile-illuminated face. I gently wiped her tears and uttered, "No more!" At which her eyes beamed bearing all the light of the world.

She fought her tears for a second, and then she broke down, eschewing everything that was pent up inside her for years, which daily hardships prevented from coming to the surface, and which added heaviness. The falling tears imparted a feather-like lightness. I hugged her, stroked her back gently, and led her inside the house.

For dinner, mother cooked my favorite *Biryani* with only four pieces of chicken, which we could afford at the cost of two days of our daily grocery then. She kept all those chicken pieces on my plate, believing that I would not know it was only four pieces. I too feigned ignorance and ate all of them, with suffering and guilt, every morsel and bite as heavy as the tears I fought back and the smile and happiness I paraded. Mother had seen good days. By eating everything myself, I, at least, affirmed her, the return of those days.

The next morning, ordinary daily words gained weight and became unutterable. The tongues refused to carry them outside. And, keeping them inside added heaviness, giving a distinct heaving sound to our breathing. Tears came and kept falling, with a sputtering sound. Among these sounds, I left home that day, in silence.

On my way to the center, I kept looking back, taking a glimpse of the mother, watched her reducing to a dot in space and vanishing, always vanishing, something of her still there, every time I looked at her, every time I look at her.

I was assigned the job of a window cleaner at the city's central hospital. Though the war was half a decade old in the nation yet, it had an air of juvenility in this particular town. The natives appeared bruised and upbeat. They believed that this war is their God's will, and it would redeem their existence as a nation, as someone who refused to budge against an enormous adversary. They said that the world would know of our courage *and lack of diplomacy*—many years later, I added in my thought.

These were the scant conversations I had with the locals. Since they were always going somewhere, they were never resting. Every now and then, a caravan, with cattle and belongings, moved somewhere. Everything appeared to be in a state of endless motion. The trees looked scorched and mostly shorn of leaves as if mourning their immobility in a place where survival was brutally tied down to one's ability to move.

How far this movement helped in surviving the war is yet to be ascertained, but it certainly gave the natives a feeling that they were doing their part in averting their annihilation. And, they could not have done more than that.

The sad trees, whom their leaves abandoned first and preferred to loiter with the air, were next disowned by the birds. They preferred to nest in deep craters and hollows of the earth. Some of them took shelter in the ruins and rubbles of the buildings. They somehow avoided the intact buildings. The war taught them their fragility and bestowed an understanding of where the safety laid.

I cleaned the windows and panes during the day. During the work break, I used to roam around the city. The debris of ornate buildings, the entwined rust and enamel glaze of mangled cars, the bullet-ridden mirror-like glass panes of the shopping arcades, the death processions, the scattered limbs, the bloodstains on the street. These images chased me life-long, competing against each other for their sole persistence in my visual memory. Not only I failed to ascertain the most horrific of them all, but I even mistook mundane bruises or shaving cuts for severed limbs or ripped bellies. The war, though visually rich, paradoxically numbed my visual judgment. It compensated for my visual impairment by honing up my aural abilities.

As evening approached, the siren used to go announcing for the residents to shelter themselves wherever they felt safe. The daily bustle of ever-moving humanity would suddenly come to a stop, and an ear-piercing silence filled the city.

The occasional barking of dogs, loud sounds of a particularly brilliant light flash, and the vagrant city winds used to breach its advances. And, sometimes, human wailings were heard too. Aided by nightly darkness and the blackouts, the silence used to assume a behemoth proportion, and nothing posed a formidable challenge to its course, except time.

During such nights, everything would slow down. Time used to stretch itself and become heavy. The clock hands moved with reluctance, becoming sluggish by the increased weight of time. I, along with two other fellow workers—Mukhiya and Nonua, often used to wake up in the middle of the night.

"Nonua, are you up?"

"Yes, never slept, actually."

"I, too, could not sleep, was just lying down and waiting for one of you to speak something."

These dialogues, more or less, we spoke to one another every night. At first, we started telling stories to each other.

"When I was in eighth grade, I fell in love."—said Nonua

"And, one day, my friends broke this news in front of the whole class," continued Mukhiya, lost in his meditations.

"The girl then mocked me and complained to the teacher, accusing me of a misdemeanor."—I used to add.

We all had similar lives and, therefore, related stories. In each story, we found traces of our own stories. And, we used to end up in our soliloquy. Isolated islands, floating in the sea of time. It used to make us indifferent to the looming time. But, occasional sounds from the city used to hurl us back into our present, where time would interrogate and mock us for our ventures into the past.

Killing time never seemed so relevant and pleasurable. We started discussing the direction, source, and cause of the sound emanating from the city.

"Dogs howled, I think."

"No, it is an old woman, whose husband's dead-body is stuck in the road tar."

"In the road tar?"

"I don't know how, but the temperature soared to such a level, making tar on the road sticky, and people who were running on them, got trapped and died.

"I have seen a body made up of tar, with its knees and arms submerged in the road."

"I know what is causing it, I have heard people talking about a fire falling from the sky. That fire does that."

"It must be then that old woman. But the howling of dogs must not be ruled out."

"Look, the woman must be trying to get her husband's body out of the tar, and the dogs must have gathered. Then, fearing an attack from them, she must have done something to the dogs, and in the act, both must have howled."

"Indeed, in war, dogs and humans struggle against each other and howl indistinguishably."

"What's that sound?"

"The gun squad shooting their traitors."

"How?"

"I clean the wall every morning."

"Ohh!"

"Yesterday, my boss took me there. While he was explaining, a man with his hands tied was brought there. He stood there facing the gun squad."

"The boss rudely told him to stand a few feet away from the wall. The wall will get less dirty now."—He added with a mocking indifference. Everybody laughed as if a joke was cracked."

"He also offered one plastic sheet to the man and made him stand over it, and with the same indifference, he pointed at me to take notice."

"He must be too bothered about the blood being *spilled*?"

One night, an exploding sound, with a brilliant flash of light, was heard. Its vibration rattled the window panes. Leaving the game in its midst, I rushed towards the window panes I used to clean. Therefore, their shattering was akin to shattering of my economic existence, and thus, my only life. I counted the number of broken window panes, with every count, I felt a part of my being getting diminished. I closed all the windows and held one of them, believing that would somehow prevent them from shaking and breaking. My impatient body shook more.

All of a sudden, a series of such sounds mauled my senses. The whole city was submerged in a bright flash. Suddenly the temperature rose, and I fainted.

When I regained consciousness, I found myself half-buried under debris, clutching a broken fragment of the window. I was pulled out and taken to the ambulance. While on my way, a journalist asked me, maybe to make his news more poignant—

"How do you feel to be carpet-bombed?"

"What…carpet bombing?"—A lost question, flattened by life, crushing the life, I thought.

"Yes, carpet bombing."

In response, I could only recite a verse of Ghalib:

"Where the body has burnt, the heart too must have been burned

Scraping the ashes, what do you search for now?"

Many years later, when wars became part of our mythology, I decided to write and publish poetry about how I felt about carpet bombing. I started submitting my work to magazines and journals. At some such time, while I was reading a magazine's submission guidelines, I came across this:

"We strongly recommend that authors familiarize themselves with recent issues before submitting. Submissions that demonstrate familiarity with the journal tend to receive more attention than those that appear to be part of a carpet-bombing campaign."

How beautiful it would have been, had poetry been used for carpet bombing?

Note: "Carpet Bombing" first appeared on *eFiction India.*

FOUR ANNAS

On every birthday, Mirza's mother gave him a four-anna coin. As a kid, he never found it odd. However, on growing up, the practice intrigued him. First, he could not understand how she managed to get a four-anna coin each year, which went out of circulation a long time ago. Secondly, and more importantly, so, four annas must have meant a lot to her; otherwise, its monetary value was not worthy of a gift. He asked her on many occasions, but she only smiled back. Mirza remained satisfied with her smile, considering it more deserving than an answer.

After Mirza's mother passed away, a series of rituals occupied him. He did not find enough time to mourn. Mirza had not even had a chance to look through her belongings—a little suitcase, nothing else. Then his birthday arrived, feeling the pangs of his mother's absence, he took out the bag. It opened in flood; its plopping sound made Mirza remember his first train journey with his mother. He saw an open, uncovered railway platform, with a dark, black rail engine chugging and whistling past it. A translucent film of smoke covered the rail's engine as if it clothed itself in a fluttering, see-through black dupatta. The smoke-filled air, as reliable as the rail's engine, painted his memory like how a deft artist colors a white sheet with charcoal. And, in this chaos, he remembered his mother opening the suitcase, the plopping sound rising as a piece of music from the noise of time, muting everything else.

For the first time, Mirza realized his mother is now no more. He began to sob. Some weight shifted in his chest, making him lighter and coherent in his world. He felt like growing up from a protected kid to an orphan adult in that brief moment, as long as the plopping lasted as if the suitcase carried not his mother's belongings, but his actual adult self. He gathered the stuff and began arranging them in the closet, making a museum to her and his childhood. There he caught hold of a clinking, rectangular, rusted tin box. The clinking sound knocked on his heart, making him curious and sure at the same time about the box's contents. Opening the box, he found many four-anna coins inside. He did not care to count them, for he knew, mother must not have counted them. The box smelt of his' mother's fragrance as if after leaving this world, she had been living in this box all along and knocked from inside to get the attention of her son. The box also had a letter. It was written on one of his birthdays. Perhaps moved by Mirza's insistence for answers, she had penned it.

You were perhaps three or four years old. Your father was away in some city, looking for a job. We lived in the village then. Living there, however, had become increasingly difficult. Crops had failed. We survived on kindness. The postman, who occasionally passed through the village, ringing his bicycle's bell, had brought no news of your father. No report was bad news, for good news carried money-orders and letters. But your father once wrote a letter that had no money-order with it. The postman had called him shameless to do so. I, however, said the letter without money was most precious to me.

"He is looking for a job and has reached out to me, sharing his failures. That's what letters are written for, and not as a note to accompany some money-orders"—I had said to the postman, salvaging my husband's pride. Unable to understand, the postman said he knew many who had gone to cities for jobs but ended up tilling Thakur's fields in their very own village.

"He is educated."—I had objected.

"Perhaps that's why he is finding it hard,"—the postman had laughed and left. I had to smile at the postman's words, though they were full of malice. It was not wise to offend him; after all, he was the one who would bring money-orders to our doors. However, in my heart, the torment lingered, until it melted into a reservoir of sadness.

No sooner had the postman left the door, the clinking of his bicycle's bell still hovering in the air, there strayed into the village a seller of plastic toys; cheap glittering necklace, rings, bangles, and animal-shaped balloons. He rode a mud smeared, rusted bicycle, which had all his wares hung around itself. He had carefully tied colorful ribbons all over the bicycle. A handful of these ribbons were left untied at one of their ends. This, along with the dangling balloons, created an impression of a large colorful fish, with a long swinging mustache, swimming through the air. If this was not enough, the seller had a bell to attract children.

The village was small, and the word got around. You, like most other children, gathered around the seller. Knowing that I would not be able to fulfill your demands, I hid behind the door and watched you from a distance. Tears also welled up.

Some children came with their parents. These were the ones he allowed to touch the toys, whisking away the others who tried to get too close. I cringed when he shoved you. I could not bear watching you from a distance, seeing you being used by someone as a prop to gain visibility by making a crowd out of you. No mother would be able to bear the nine months, if she ever comes to know this tragic fate awaits her kid, that her kid is no longer an individual, no longer possessing the traits she passed on, no longer displaying the etiquettes she taught him, but merely a part of the crowd, faceless and unrecognizable. Helpless, I closed the door behind me and sat there motionless. I did not move in what felt like hours. My mind drifted off to Karbala. I found myself humming a *marsiya*, putting into tune the suffering of Rubab, and dissolving my own within it. I knew that I would overcome the pain, if only I could imagine the plight of Rubab who lost her six-month-old baby, Ali, when an arrow pierced his parched throat. While everyone was deciding who would get what, your cousins with their parents also gathered there. I could hear their voices. I had some hope; maybe they would buy you something.

I began looking from the cracks in the door. You were looking at your cousins with the balloons in their hands. Your uncles bargained with the seller to give you a balloon for free, saying that they had already bought five from him. The seller, however, was unmoved. Your uncles convinced that they had fulfilled their duty of kinship, began returning to their homes. I thought of coming out, but our conditions then were such that my presence would have implied an obligation for your uncles. I felt they were always happier when we were not involved.

Around then, you snatched the balloon from Azad's hand and burst it in the ensuing scuffle. Your uncle was enraged and slapped you in the rage. I could not bear the sight anymore and rushed to you. I almost cried, but something inside prevented me. I tried hard to toughen up my face while the pain shipwrecked inside me. When it became unbearable, I thrashed you, muttering gibberish. To appear proud, I asked your uncle, in a breathless voice, the price of the balloon. I was hoping that he would say not to worry about it. But he had replied four annas.

Mirza felt as if someone had stamped his soul with a searing four-anna coin. It carried with itself guilt, shame, anger, and humiliation, like an infection to the wound. How much four annas had meant to his mother, he realized. How little his wealth now would add up to that four annas, he reflected.

Mirza read the letter more than once. The first time he felt something stirred inside him. The following readings brought some understanding to him. How seemingly small events sit inside the void within us, he wondered. He took out a few coins from the box in his hand, as one takes a fistful of water from a river. He tried to feel the weight of the coins, by moving his hand slightly up and down, as a measure to weigh something inexpressible, unseen. Perhaps he found them lighter. He rose immediately and vanished out of the room. He appeared a few minutes later, holding another box in his hand. He opened the box and poured its contents into his mother's box. The four-anna coins fell in a rush, making a dull, vibrant sound as if someone was speaking Spanish. These were the coins he had received from his mother so far, keeping each of them, safely. He once again felt the box in his palm to feel the weight. Though it increased, he was still unsatisfied, as if he wished something else to happen out of this act, as if the weight would help him unravel the mystery of life and death, that he may be able to hold his mother again in his hand. He felt the heaviness inside as if the coins had filled his heart. He shut the box and the closet and rose sluggishly from there, only to walk with a gait that looked as if he was carrying some invisible weight within himself. At this moment, after roughly a month had passed, he felt his mother's absence. He realized that the lack is such a large house that one can actually fly a kite in its air; it is so transparent that one can walk through its wall. Unable to cope up with the sudden vastness of his modest house, caused by the feeling of his mother's absence, he went outside, into the street. The clinking sound of bicycles poured into his ears and brought a smile on his face. He began walking toward the sound.

Note: "Four Annas" first appeared on the *Ethos Literary Journal.*

A Sailor's Journey

Darkness fades from the sky. The night slips out of the tenuous hold of time—like a snake sheds its skin—a patch of gleam, but mostly dull. New dawn descends along the shore. A sleepy sailor sets on his boat. The boat has few holes—family and friends fill them, and hand him a pair of oars. Half-asleep, the sailor pushes the boat into the choppy sea, and bids farewell to his people left behind on the island.

Someone once told him that no place belongs to anyone until a loved one is buried in its soil. The belongingness of the sailor is even more profound. The soil itself is his soul, his heart, the tender earth of the island.

Tears well up in the sailor's eyes, and immediately retreat inside. The earth within becomes softer. At such an occasion, time often stays put with a handful of seeds in its hand. And once the agony of separation, with its pulsating force, has tilled the moist heart, time scatter these seeds, to grow them into a forest.

A similar forest of memories would soon start to grow in the sailor's heart. It is in this forest he would be lost looking for his island. The sailor will reach new lands, but forever he would look for what is buried and grows inside him—his island.

The sailor starts to moan. The people ask him not to do it. They shout, "It is a sea journey, you will need water ahead, sip these then, save these tears." For the journey, the sailor saves his tears.

The turbulent sea makes the sailor fearful. The salty water slaps him from all sides, and gets into his eyes, making them burn. The sailor takes out a few drops of water from his eyes and cleans them. The burning gets better. The tears, while carefully avoiding the wind, start to draw parallel lines on the sailor's cheeks. What begins as a child's play soon becomes a race. The wind distorts the straight lines and laughs. The sailor hears the laughter but is unable to make much sense of it. The drops tire soon. They rest on the lips and slither inside the mouth. The sailor sighingly swallows them.

The wind is a thing of its own. It is obviously wind, just a form of air, breathable, but also with an odor and taste. It weights itself as if some personality. And, likewise, the wind travels with an entourage, carrying along with salty crystals, mist, and an unusual heat. Birds appear rather trapped within this wind than flying on their own free will.

The bulky movement gives the wind a distinct density. One gets a feeling of being slapped wherever the wind touches. The wind's higher density makes the sailor inhale a smaller breath to be comfortable. But on a sea journey, the metaphor is not lost on him, that the sailor must pay due respect to whatever natural element he encounters. Therefore, the sailor takes a shallower breath, not only out of respect but also out of fear, feeling that if he breathes too much of this heavy air, he may drown.

The journey reaches a stage where it is necessary to sleep, to dream. The sailor attempts but fails. His dreams are only memories. Few pictures of his past life, hurriedly put together. The sailor grows restless. Not because he is unable to sleep or dream—he no longer can make sense of his memories. He cannot say if his memories are real or imagined. He decides to sew, with his own hands, the fabric of his memories. But the sailor entangles himself in choosing the thread. Whether it is blue or red, he fails to decide the color of the memories. Alone, his recollection fails. Finally, he settles with a few black and white threads.

When the sailor is busy sewing his minds, the holes, his people filled, are undone. The water begins flooding the boat. The fabric, still half-sewn, the sailor uses to fill the gaps. He squeezes water from the cloth and returns it to the sea. Some drops he puts on his lips. But the sea dislikes the soiling of its sacrament. She punishes the sailor by drawing water out of his heart.

Now even his breath is salty. He smells like the sea. The journey is not only bringing the sailor closer to his destination but also stuffing him with itself. By the time the sailor would reach his place, he would become a journey in himself. A sea would forever move within his veins, rousing in him a desire to return, and when unable to do so, he would then resort to travel within himself, searching for this sea, whose sound the sailor would hear in his dreams, whose smell he would forever feel. After he would die and rest in the earth, the salinity of the soil would increase, some crystals would gleam at his grave, and the air near it will have a salty flavor.

By dusk, destination appears at the far edge of the sea. The boat half-filled with water gets to the shore. The sailor steps out of his ship as if rising from his grave. Two guards accost him. Ask the sailor why he is here, when he would return, etc.. The sailor turns back and looks to his land left behind. He sees, or perhaps imagines seeing, his family and friends. All as silhouettes. He imagines the feature of their faces. He sees a wait in their eyes.

As if imagination caused some heat, the sailor's eyes begin to melt. His heart, which had hardened from the journey, suddenly felt like a water-filled balloon, soft and squishy. I will return tomorrow, the sailor says. The sailor feels the taste of the salt as he speaks. The crushing of crystals gives a resonant tone to his voice. The resulting lilt in the sailor's speech pleases the guards. They immediately believe him and welcome him to their island. The sailor enters the island and starts preparing for the journey back home.

The sun begins to move elsewhere. While parting its way, the sun planted a kiss on the lips of the sky, making the sky blush. The resulting diffused pinkish glow welcomed the first ray of darkness. A curtain, studded with moon and stars, starts to fall. The night takes back the stage.

The night knows, just as all other natural elements are aware, as they have been doing it since eternity that no journey is complete until the traveler returns to where he has started. And then the cycle goes on, endlessly, for one never knows where one had started—only those who learn to travel within get some respite.

Note: "A Sailor's Journey" first appeared in *The Punch Magazine*.

AN INCIDENT IN THE CHEMISTRY LAB

"Hey, silver guy!" Sitting at my desk, pretending to do something, I was startled. The department chair stood before me. They call you the silver guy?—he gloated as if calling Bruce Wayne, Batman. Yes, Sir, some graduate students do. I replied matter-of-factly. This deflated the playfulness in his voice. I work on silver recovery from the laundry wash water. Great! That's great—he heaped praise, in a way, affected and precisely American. Saying a prosaic thank-you-Sir, I watered down his enthusiasm. His lips then folded together and pressed against his cheeks. He nodded his head a couple of times. And then, reached into his pockets. He was holding a piece of medallion to me. Perhaps, of silver.

This I want you to clean. I looked at the medallion. It had a lady's face etched onto it. You want me to remove these black marks. Hoon-

hoon—he sounded. Can you do this for me? Sure, I can do this. I knew its chemistry. I began preparing the solution. He stood there, looking at me doing the task. What are you mixing? Tell me? I did not answer him. I simply smiled. His question took me to an incident during my school days.

I am in class 8th. Our class is in the chemistry lab. There is no teacher around. I see bottles of nitric acid, hydrochloric acid. I begin mixing them, attempting to make *aqua regia*. I had read before: it is nitric acid and hydrochloric acid mixed in a certain ratio and used for cleaning precious metals. A senior student stands next to me, saying repeatedly—*Bata na, bata na kya kar raha hai (Hey! What are you up to?)*.

"Nothing, nothing, you have your keys? I'll clean it for you."

Perhaps, wary of my claims, he doesn't give me his. I find some nails, rusted ones, and put them in the solution. Brown fumes and pungent smell start filling the lab. I'm delighted. More because it entertains my other friends. Their faces elicit awe and admiration for me or maybe, to the reaction unfolding before them. However, this curiously jacks me up. Their facial features are what fame is made up of—at least the alluring side of it. Therefore, to deepen the feeling, I amble for some more material to throw inside the fuming solution. I find a battery and toss it in. The reaction attains some vigor, feebly matching our collective curiosity. There are calls to add some more stuff to it. However, they all fade away when Dr. Naqvi, our Chemistry teacher, enters the lab, roaring—.*acid kisney use kiya (Who took the acid?)*? His words have magical effects.

Everyone disappears, leaving me in some sort of void, where only I stand with the bottle of acid in my hand. Dr. Naqvi stands in front of me, seething. You-criminal-get-out-of-this-lab-you-will-never-enter-here-get-out-you-criminal-you-are-criminal. His words surface in such quick successions as if sewn together—as if his tongue hides the thread and needle—as if someone stitches them together. I whimper with a customary apology. It fails. It won't work— I knew it. Everyone knew it. However, it is necessary; otherwise, I will curse myself that I did not try enough. More importantly, it would ensure that when his calm returns and the concerned authority would carry on with its regular chores, such apology would be the starting point to broach the subject and settle it within the limits of its physical effects. Yes, physical effects, if you consider character impressions beyond the purview of physicality. You-go-stand-outside-you-will-stand-here-for-all-times-to-come-you-are-criminal. He physically pushes me outside. I don't take his actions or words to heart. For indeed, I'm aware of my ill-doings, if not criminality, and above all, Dr. Naqvi has helped me on several counts before.

I stand outside, while the lab resumes working, perhaps, more seriously now. I hear no classroom hum that typically lingers. Mr. Ali is coming from somewhere. He is the lab assistant and teaches us chemistry. Seeing me outside, he thinks I am just loafing around—a*ur bhai, tu yahan kya kar raha hai, chal andar* (*Oh, hero! What's up? Come along.*). Mr. Ali has this non-formal, rustic way of talking. This endears him to us. I think he knows it well and enjoys it. He will interfere on our behalf or ignore whenever we are found wanting in terms of specific rules and regulations like on several occasions he finds us out of bounds but has never reported to the teacher-in-charge.

I tell him what happened. I urge him to help me in making peace with Dr. Naqvi. He assures me saying—*chal dekhta hoon* (*Okay, I'll see to it.*). Earlier, I have helped Mr. Ali with his *KBC preparations.* Therefore, he could not have refused me. Moments later, Mr. Ali comes outside: c*hal, sorry bol de, aur aaeenda se nahi kariyo, chal aja* (*Listen, get into the lab. Say sorry and pledge not to repeat the same.*). I approach Dr. Naqvi and apologize. Dr. Naqvi, though still livid, doesn't call me criminal anymore. He calls me a good student. He is my housemaster, too; therefore, he brings my parents in the conversation. He reminds me of their hopes. I listen to him intently and promise that I would never do this again. He asks me to join the class. Mr. Ali follows me as I get in. I turn to him and say, thank you. He gloats— *main na hota to pata nahi tera kya hota* (*How you guys will manage without me?*). Some of my classmates, whom I look at, are smiling. I smile, betraying the remorse I had only moments ago.

It's challenging to be remorseful at that age. I never felt it back then. Even surfacing on our faces while making an apology, the remorse was never real. It was always a means to lessen punishments for our trespasses, if not avoiding them. And, in our calculus, the punishments were never a logical outcome of any of our deeds. They were part of our acts, something unavoidable, even necessary. We accepted them with smug resignation, if not stoically. The punishment meted out to us only meant delay, interruptions, maybe even diversions, to our final goals. Once it got over, we would continue doing what we were doing in its absence. Therefore, when the lab period began coming to an end, and a rush for submitting the lab files ensued. I got hold of two fresh bottles of acids, whose names I did not care to look at, and hid them in the bushy mass outside the lab after everyone was gone. I secretly went there and brought the bottles to the barber's shed. My classmates helped me in hiding them in an abandoned pipeline next to the generator room. The next day, early morning, I cleaned my keys and demonstrated it in the classroom. The sparkle in my classmates' eyes testified and multiplied the sparkling my keys possessed. By the evening playtime, I had quite a handful of keys to clean.

As I sat there, next to the generator room, cleaning the blackened keys, restoring their sheen, under the curious glare of my classmates, I felt like some druid, making some magic potion. I was smiling—a pure smile. But this time, cleaning the

Professor's medallion, my smile had something more. It had a tenderness that usually comes from recollecting a fond memory.

The Professor again went on—tell me what you have mixed. I said, removing my gas mask, revealing a smile beneath— "memories." I offered him his cleaned, shining medallion.

Note: "An Incident in the Chemistry Lab" first appeared in *Oakgrovians*, an alumni portal of Oak Grove School, Mussoorie.

A Reunion

My God, my God, who am I watching? How many am I? Who is I? What is this gap between me and myself?
—Fernando Pessoa
The Book of Disquiet

I left my home at a very tender age. It was not some philosophical wandering—the one associated with the search for meaning. It was the pre-determined path of my time. The track was set before my birth. And, a dream was erected at its center—a goal that was less personal than societal. Every individual of my time was expected to do *whatever it takes* to make it come true. This was the most significant upheaval of my time. It took me to different places and uprooted me from there on numerous pretexts.

First, I left my home for education. The kind of education that pushed me farther away from my true nature and instilled in me a raw, primal instinct for survival. After school, it took me to different places for jobs and then for endless other jobs. At these places, it not only uprooted me but also scattered me. Every place I left, snatched part from me. The fragments continued living at these places even when I was long gone from them. My existence extended not only in time but also in space—broken shards strewn all over. My countless finitude escaped even my own recognition. All the broken lives I kept wandering for completion. I visited and re-visited places looking for them. And sometimes, my little fragmented lives too came looking for their real selves. We mutually haunted one another. Sometimes we spent time together, sharing our tiny isolated tales. Even then, we only had a vague feeling of belongingness, which we could never explicitly express. Such was the fragmentation life and dreams caused to us.

Then one day, I died by suicide.

It was a confession that life is too much for me. Or, as Camus puts it in everyday words, it *"is not worth the trouble."* It is not that I did it without contemplation. I reflected a lot. *If I leave a place, I carry with me a part of that place, but I also leave a fragment of mine there. What happens to that fragment if I die?* This question always occupied me.

During my time, it was fashionable to take spiritual diversions. It was a fad. People believed that it would take the stress out of the daily routine and increase efficiency at work. I too dabbled in it. And thus, the notion of the afterlife flowered. It was then I decided to confess that life *is not worth the trouble.*

It was an erroneous decision.

The spiritual promise of the afterlife was not without its terms and conditions—Mother Nature told me. She was an implacable and dispassionate being. She told me that life flowed like a stream and not as isolated drops. In its flow, it touches the shores of birth and death. She assured that the streams—out of affection or repulsion—do not always reach the beaches, but strike them with violence and fragment themselves into tiny drops. But she insisted that these drops must coalesce to merge into the ocean of life. I tried to win her through logic—a tool mastered in my time with imbecile perfection. But sadly, Mother Nature detests reasonings.

Death, therefore, did not put closure to my agonies. It spawned the whole set of afterlives that almost resembled the earlier life. In life, I doubted the life, and in death, I questioned the death. And, after experiencing both, the difference between the two is muddled.

Death did not change anything. After a brief pain, it restored the earlier life I had. But didn't I suffer pain when I took birth?

With everyone and everything similarly intact as in life, I live my normal life in death. I carry out all my earlier tasks. And everyone else too exists as before. Sometimes, I forget that I am dead, as I used to forget to be alive during my lifetime. But, in solitude, a feverish nostalgia for unity overwhelms me. I move restlessly in my cities, looking for my other fragments. Sometimes we find each other. A primordial sense of belongingness draws us close. Then we share our tales. The forgetfulness takes over, not like the prevalent phenomena of shrinking memory caused by too much information consumption. Still, more like sleep, the kind necessary to *live*, that lulls the unresolvable inconsistencies and renders *life* bearable. And then, we part, believing the meeting to be a delusion—a result of some fervent hope. But, one day, something happened.

It was a lazy Friday afternoon. I was at home. I had had breakfast and was lying in the balcony. The gentle caresses of sunlight were making me warm. An occasional spurt of cold wind made the excessive warmth tolerable. *The Short Stories* by Maupassant was resting on my chest. My eyes were grazing the lyrical prose. The words streamed through my consciousness like a mother's lullaby. It dulled my senses. After a while, it spread over my face and stayed there. I began to relax. The long-held weariness was dissipating from my pores. Sleep was around the corner. The eyelids had begun to acquire weight.

"It's time. Get ready."

I heard the mother saying. The voice seemed distant—broken and distorted.

She came nearer. I could sense her. Yet the voice remained all too far. Sleep by that time had usurped my sense of hearing.

Nearness between people can sometimes be measured by how close to themselves they sense each other's voices. This, I reflected in my stupor. It helped me to overhear the mother and slip back to the embracing world of sleep.

"There's hardly any time left."

"The water is ready, bathe, and go for the prayer."

"Nobody cares for prayers these days."

The emotional measure of the voice was getting distinct. It had begun to pierce through the barrier I constructed to disregard the surroundings. The indifference necessary for sleeping began to fade away. And each passing moment successively pushed me towards consciousness.

I removed *The Short Stories* by Maupassant. The sunlight fiercely invaded my eyes. The assault lasted for a few seconds. I laid there motionless and waited for another nudge from the mother. The mother gently slapped me at the back. I got up. The mother with a towel in her hand was standing in front of me.

"I have been standing here for the past hour. Don't I have other works to do?"

I smiled and said—"The father was right when he used to say that you always exaggerate your work and number of hours you put into them." What I said was unimportant and was done more to supplant a smile on her face. It worked. It has always worked. The mother's mood lightened. Her face beamed with a smile. It multiplied the falling sunlight. It brightened up the surrounding and made it feather-light. Smile and sunshine fused into each other. They became indiscernible. My sleepiness vanished. I rubbed my eyes a few times. It did away with whatever remained of the sleep —a few moments ago that seemed almost deathly.

I got up and began to prepare for the weekly Friday prayer. I did this to appease my mother rather than out of any religious consideration. Maybe others do the same.

I took the warm water which the mother prepared and went to have my bath. The warm water was comforting. It restored the sleepiness to an extent. I dozed off in between. The mother knocked on the door. I opened and found her standing just outside the door with all my dresses. I came out and began to dress up.

I occasionally kept looking at the placidly moving wall clock. It did not appear threatening, unlike the ones I am used to. The wall clock at home has always been benign. It tells time and only when sought. It rarely seeks attention. Its ticking sound conveys the rhythmic breathing of home. And when I have accidentally awakened in the middle of the night, the continuous ticking has lulled me back to a reassuring homely sleep. After I have started working, I have come to treat it as one of the family members. And I always pay my gratitude with a smile every time I look at it.

After dressing up, I went to the mother and told her that I would be leaving now. The mother then turned over the various coversheets that laid over the refrigerator, dining table, T.V. top, and the bookshelf. She moved her hand over them and brought forth numerous coins of almost every existent denomination. She always saves these coins and keeps them safe for distributing as alms. Every day, little by little, she remembers the poor folks in her thoughts and actions. The mother gave me a few coins and asked me to distribute them to the poor who would gather at the prayer. I pocketed everything and headed to the nearest mosque.

A sea of footwears greeted me at the mosque entrance. I added mine to them. Inside the mosque, everyone else seemed to stare at everyone else. The gaze carried either an interrogating curiosity or a gloating statement about one's loyalty. To me, a Friday prayer has always appeared more like a guilt-lessening session than actual worship, where people come to repent their week-long forgetfulness of worship and return somewhat guilt-free. I never found this notion repulsive but ridiculous.

After a brief struggle, I failed to find a space to pray. I absolved myself of further effort and stood at the far end. It did not bother me. But it certainly bothered someone in front of me. He pushed some of the kids from his row behind and asked me to join. I felt terrible for the kids. Considering it to be a norm, I chose not to resist and accepted the space he provided.

The new space was by the window. I sat there for a while and waited for the prayer's final call. On the sounding of the last call, I rose with the congregation. While standing up, something at the window sill caught my attention.

It was a copy of *The Myth of Sisyphus*.

It was kept inverted and opened, signifying the reader's intent to resume reading from where he left. The whetted curiosity made the prayer unbearable. The whole time I remained fixated with the idea of meeting the reader. It was not only joyous anticipation of meeting a fellow reader but also a feverish feeling of meeting someone of your own kind. A kind that grapples with the meaning of existence. And in its pursuit, straddles divine and blasphemous territories. A thrill associated with an unexpected meeting of members of some secret sect in public took over me.

My prayer lost its rhythm. I merely performed the routineness of the act. After the prayer, groveling invocations for divine blessing commenced. It seemed longer than the prayer itself. The Imam's voice quivered and reached the point of wailing. After this role play, he was found gloating and beaming with a face that betrayed the howling voice that sought divine blessings moments ago.

The people rushed to move out. An intense earnestness for reaching home was palpable everywhere. Everything, in the end, contradicted the message of peace, contentment, and grace delivered in the sermon. On other Fridays, this would have been my moment of resolving not to come the next time. But this time, my thoughts were glued to the book and its owner. I drew closer to the book and held it in my hand. I started reading the marked page.

"That nostalgia for unity, that appetite for the absolute illustrates the essential impulse of the human drama."

An unusual force emanating from the smell of the wrinkled pages of the book hurled me somewhere deep within me. A whispering voice with old age stamped all over it broke my reverie.

"This book says that suicide is the only earnest philosophical question."

I turned and found him sitting on the floor. His face exuded light. His smile quivered like a candle flame flickering in an airy night. I drew closer to him. His hand trembled when he made gestures. By the motion of his worn-out hand, he asked me to sit on the floor with him. He asked, "You like this book?"

Before nodding in affirmative, I noticed that his words sweetened the air surrounding us like a sweet, mild fragrance of a perfume, which always remains in a state of dying—one that caresses the senses but does not revolt against them.

"You can take it and return after reading. I have read it several times."

"Thank you. I have read it once."

"Then you should read it once more, even twice, maybe thrice. You don't just read a book, you read into yourself too. These fixed words are the least static of things you can expect in this nature. I would suggest you read it once more."

He continued. His voice gained strength. His smile quivered less. He appeared younger now.

"You know Jorge Luis Borges?" He did not wait for my reply and continued.

"Borges, in one of his stories, said that a book is best to read the second time."

He paused as if he wanted to say something, but his memory failed him. In those brief moments, he aged again. All his fervent ways vanished. His shoulders stooped. He began to pick words again in his quivering ways.

"I don't remember the exact title, but I do have some vague memories of its content. The protagonist had only one book."

He again seemed to struggle with his memories. He began speaking diffidently. His voice began to reflect his old age again. His hand pressed his forehead. Believing it would spill out the details from his head. It helped.

In a broken voice, he said, "He had *Iliad* or maybe some Shakespearean work. I don't remember well. Forgive my old age." A sense of shame was visible.

He continued—"The protagonist one day meets a young man who has read a lot of books. They discuss books and reading. I don't remember the whole discussion clearly, but the upshot is that reading a book several times distills numerous meanings of the same tale. It may make you realize about your multiple existences."

Speaking thus, he almost reached the limits of his breath. He panted and concluded everything by saying, "You understand what I mean?"

With his words, the sea inside me that was long frozen tumbled. An ancient forgotten desire came alive. But I could not make sense of these rumblings at that time. I dismissed them as a sign of exhaustion and nodded in agreement.

With this, a pause followed. A break that is often associated with conversations among strangers who have just lost or exhausted the context. We both sat there for a while, groping for an escape—from each other, or maybe from the pervading silence that roamed between us.

After a while, the silence condensed and fell like drops. The conversation ensued again. We began by exchanging a few social niceties that made the mutual strangeness bearable and helped explore a shared space. The conversation meandered to a point where a sense of mutual trust developed. A feeling of meeting someone long-lost grew.

He asked me to accompany him to his room located on the top of the mosque. He tried to get on his feet. I took his arms, put them over my shoulders, and helped him stand. We then walked to the top. His gait reminded me of a book opened by a furious wind. A gale of fluttering and then a moment of pause. Interlude of quick, wavering steps and then moments of rest. Walking, holding, and resting briefly after every few steps, we reached his room.

At the door, he waited for a while, as if measuring out the pros and cons of bringing a stranger to his room. Still unsure of himself, he gave in to the prevailing inertia and pushed the door gently. The door gave way to the inside with its universal creaking. The room smelled of burnt flesh and papers. Settled ashes moved with hesitation. A mat was spread in the center, and a steel trunk was kept at the corner of the room. The room appeared inhabited and forsaken at the same time.

"What happened here?"

He stretched over the mat, motionless, looked straight at the ceiling, secretly decanted his thoughts, passed them through the filter of reflection, and burst open in poetry.

> I speak for you, companions on a journey
> Dense, not devoid of effort,
> And also for you who have lost
> The soul, the spirit, the wish to live.
> Or nobody or somebody, or perhaps only one, or you
> Who are reading me: remember the time
> Before the wax hardened,
> When each one of us was like a seal.
> Each of us carries the imprint
> Of the friend met along the way;
> In each the trace of each.

The lyrical cadence of his reply moved me. However, meanings took birth after a while. And it further took some more moments before my response breached the prevailing calm of the poetical utterance.

"Beautiful!"

It came out more than said. I did not wish to spear the hum the poetry created in its wake.

"Primo Levi, from *To My Friend*. This is one of my favorites."

Then he went over to the steel trunk. He brought it near the mat, opened it, and began taking out all the books. He then began to pile them up in the center of the room. Kafka, Pessoa, Borges, Tolstoy, Camus looked prominent. It added warmth and brilliance to the room. My eyes remained fixated on him, watching him with attention all these while. He touched the books as if feeling a newborn, with delicacy, warmth, and love.

The sight of these books brought forth in me the memories of all my life. In their fragrance, I could smell the time, and the places went by. In the folds of their pages, I found the experiences I had left behind. In their wrinkles, I could see the contours of all my faces. By merely seeing them, I traveled through time and space. For the first time, I could feel the magnified nature of my existence.

He kept spreading the books with deft precision and absorbed silence of a conjurer. He then constructed a mound and spread himself over it.

Fixing his gaze at me, he said—

"I lost my soul at a very young age. I was born in a time when the majority of young people were losing their souls, without knowing why. Then I grew up, pursuing what I was reared to pursue—a dream, more of a social act than an individual's will."

"Then, somewhere, at some point in time, I lost my soul."

"My existence felt passage of pain, but everyone around me approved of it. Wasn't the dream more important? And, wasn't all of us had done, or was to do the same?"

He continued after a pause—

"It was a suicide that my soul committed, more out of hope than despair."

"It is not that the soul kept me unaware of its plan, but I did not care much. Maybe my apathy made the decision easier."

"Then I aged and shriveled."

"The dream remained distant, though I achieved many of its fragments. But the process fragmented me more."

"Broken lives."

"And then, one day, while slithering through life, I decided to collect all my beings that got shattered by the dreams. And, by the time life announced its death sentence, I had managed to concentrate all my existences in my aging body."

"After I died, I became unbearably heavy."

"Mother Nature came but refused to take me inciting her own laws. She said that the soul is the wing with which the body rises and flies. Mother Nature abhors heaviness and makes things fall. I fell into the abyss."

He stared blankly at the walls, paused, and began speaking again—

"I have always cloved reading, despite losing my soul. Maybe reading tricked me into believing that I have one. Maybe that is why I gravitated towards it—to compensate for the lost soul."

"But, in this damned afterlife, even reading did not help much."

"Then, one day, Cicero told me—*A room without books is like a body without a soul.* This dictum appealed to my longings."

"I assembled all my books in this room, hoping my soul would return. I waited for thousands of years. Every evening I sit on its mound, awaiting the setting sun that passes through my window."

"Every single day, it burns me and my books with its blaze. Every evening it vaporizes me, yet every evening, I fail to fly. I just cling to this earth, like the haze that this room reeks of."

"And today, when I saw you at the mosque, your probing eyes searching for some lost self in those pages. At that moment, I felt reunited with an old lost friend. A friend in whose waiting, I have spent numerous evenings burning myself."

Speaking thus, he broke down—I could see my own teary eyes reflected in his tears.

His words unlocked the numerous prison cells inside me—selves within selves accumulated in layers of time and space run amok. I held him in an embrace, and everyone started to spill over, deluging the room, sweetening it with the fragrance of reunion. We flowed and flowed unto me—the bigger self. Spilling and tumbling, I met the wellspring.

Note: "A Reunion" first appeared in the *Indian Review*.

WINTER CAME EARLY

Winter came in the morning. It occurred sometime around midnight. He was sleeping then. Or, as he puts it—weaving his dreams. He often uses such poetical tricks to force upon his thoughtful side, on a few acquaintances he has. In reality, he was busy sleeping then, recuperating from his day's work, preparing himself for yet another day of patterned chores and timely activities.

Winter, maybe because it was untimely, came furtively inside his room, through a narrow window opening. He intentionally keeps his window slightly agape, to allow morning light to seep and invade his eyes, in case the alarm clock fails to maul his senses.

Winter began to caress his warm, exposed flesh, gently. Feeble shivering ran through his body. He forsook his half-woven dreams and hurled himself to awareness. It was dark then. He failed to identify winter lurking, diffusing inside his room. He attributed his shivering to his poor diet and daily fatigue. He turned to the other side of the bed and slept shivering.

Winter was cold. It needed warmth. Winter clung to his body and began devouring its heat. It had sucked out heat even from thick mattresses and heavy wooden chairs—beings such as these which largely remain unimpressed and indifferent to usual winter's overtures.

Before the morning could come or the alarm clock would croak, his sound of heavy breathing woke him up. By that time, winter, who came with the shyness of a leper forcibly sent to a social gathering, had assumed the ownership of his house. It was whiplashing his exposed flesh, making him shiver every time.

Stooped and quivering, he went over to his window. He sensed the wintry air. The sudden arrival of winter confounded him, almost without meaning. He, however, did not insist on one. It was acceptable in his times. Pressing for the purpose was taboo and, more importantly, childish. It was only sought to explain the most straightforward, safest phenomena.

He looked up in the sky, and quite strangely, looked into it, for nothing was up there. No moon, no stars. The air seemed vaporous. He found it fleeing away. He had known nothingness associated with the sky, of nights when he had stared above, nothingness had stared back at him, but now, wherever he looked at, nothing returned him his gaze, the sky simply moved away, revealing yet another shifting layer of nothingness, which avoided his stare as if ashamed of some untold conspiracy.

The sun, too, was late in its coming. And, when it did come, it lacked its youthful exuberance, probably for the first time showed signs of fatigue of the journey it daily makes to arrive at his window.

The subdued sun was disconcerting. He, vaguely, understood, by then, that winter has come. He now only needed a factual confirmation, maybe a news report. Feeling of cold, though important, in his times, is inadequate, and can be dismissed unless a piece of news approves it. Such feelings are even insufficient to prepare him for the coming winter, for it requires specific dresses, and unless everyone wears them, he will find them hard to put on. Still, he can put them on during nights, but in daylight, he conforms to the prevailing behavior and manners. He often expresses this contradiction in his poetry. Once he wrote:

> What darkness of night reveals
> The deceptive daylight hides
> Is a twenty-first-century man
> A time hidden from his times

Some who understood had laughed, and some who did not, also laughed. For, in his times, laughter conveys understanding.

The shifting sky arrested his gaze and kept it motionless for a while, his eyes, reflecting nothingness, reflected sky. Two emptiness united by a conduit of vision. A series of burring sound broke his reveries. It emanated from his mobile phone. It was a weather alert. Winter was now confirmed. A foreboding took him over. However, it suddenly vanished, when the same mobile phone, owing to its design, wished him a pleasant Sunday morning. He stood motionless, recollecting his days, when he had no mobile phone, and how he used to reach his workplace even on holidays, and used to return, somewhat relieved, on being revealed that the office is closed.

A satisfied smile adorned his face. However, he was more thankful to winter, for its unforeseen kindness by choosing to come on a Sunday morning. Last year it caught him unaware, in the evening, while he was returning from the office. The next day his efficiency at work had gone down.

By coming on Sunday, winter allowed him to prepare for days ahead. He quickly opened his closet and took out all his woolen garments. They were musty and needed washing before being worn. He collected them in one bag. He gathered all his other clothes for laundry. He forgot his shivering. He felt a surge of energy within him. Sunday was coming alive as an idea, where man distances himself from his daily chores, prepares to groom his inner and outer worlds, pushing boredom away, making life exciting and bearable for the rest of the week.

Winter also saved his few bucks on a haircut. He avoids haircuts during winters. He puts on a woolen cap to hide his growing hair. And, even if he removes his cap, prolonged wearing makes the hair flat and fixed. Though he looks funny, that's okay with him.

The saved money, although paltry, kept him indecisive for a while. He vacillated between purchasing old books from Mr. Cohen, who sells books in the downtown on Sundays or getting himself a few pieces of fried chicken from Caesar's. The dilemma, as an assured indecisiveness, remained on his face when he left for the launderette.

Note: "Winter Came Early" first appeared in *Flash Fiction Magazine*.

REFUGEE

She is fleeing her homeland. Not out of desire, but to survive. She is not nameless, yet a name robs her of the unique identity that she shares with many, who had earlier fled, or who are fleeing, and who will escape until the fag end of time. Refugees are a race of their own. They move in space and settle in time.

She is packing her bags she will carry for the journey and hard times peering at her. She has acquired a sudden adeptness at judging the usefulness of her belongings. This one goes there. That one is left scattered. She occasionally stops and holds some of her belongings in her hand for too long. By too long, one should not infer a period of a minute or so. Given the pace of the events surrounding her, a couple of seconds are enough to reach her decisions.

When nostalgia grips her hand, she takes moments to relive the memory associated with the concerned belongings. She moves on, but not without sighing. With each sigh, she feels an increase in the weight of memories, for she believes that sighing sucks out the past trapped in those physical objects. She has less understanding of time—for, with each passing moment, the past itself gets buried in her, making her a mound of time.

Suddenly, she becomes aware of her condition. The weight of memories is compromising her movements. She looks for one thing, in which she will put all that weight. The metaphorical spade, as some would say, to dig the mound of time. But how fruitful is digging of time? When with each digging, there is a disturbance in the contours of time and, thus, the past. It isn't past a total of past, present, and beyond? Past, with time, changes.

She is beholden by a sudden desire to return, in time and space. One would say, what a travesty, an urge to get back to a place, where she already is, and which she would soon forsake. But, that is how nostalgia, a child born out of wedlock, between time, space and the individual, works, preserving past in its sheen and pristine, making it a home in time, to which a traveler forever travels to return and take refuge. Forever travels…

She acts on her desire, for a refugee's actions are not entirely shorn of inner desires, and we must not strip of whatever residual free will is left in her. She makes the selection and swiftly moves on.

She now divides her jewelry into two parts. The more valuable ones, she carefully seals in a piece of dirty cloth, as if conferring on them a cloak of invisibility, against the prying eyes of bandits and other such creatures, whom she expects to meet in her journey ahead. She knows her trick to be old and would be exposed, by the discerning eyes, for they would know where and what to search. Yet, she goes ahead with it, acting on a slim hope, which for her, a refugee, is a reason enough to work. The purity of a refugee's faith is unmatched.

She hides the sealed jewelry in one of her bags, the one she would put under her head as a pillow for restful sleep. An object that will help, by its form—and deny, by the quality of its contents, her sleep at the same time. If the contents of the bag are not enough to make her attentive during her somnolent hours, she will loop the straps of the bag around her neck and armpit, making it a noose, which will tighten, if the bag is covetously pulled, hurling her to awareness in an instant. A refugee has to foresee the direst of consequences.

She is now wearing all her inexpensive jewelry—those are not out of fashion, but to be noticeable to the greedy eyes of some officials, and to offer them, when need be, in return of some favors, for favors would be few and seekers, many.

And, when she reaches her destination, if any such thing would ever exist for her, she will deck herself and other members of her family, with all her jewelry. She cannot afford to keep them in some hotel room or whatever.

And then, she will sleep, with an actual pillow, adorning all her jewelry, and not the other way round. Should anyone rouse her and ask, where are you, she would reply, I am in such and such place, always naming her hometown, one way or another, for she drifts back there. Because, she is traveling even in her sleep. A refugee never rests.

Note: "Refugee" first appeared in *Temper Literary Review*.

A Suicide Note

There is but one truly serious philosophical problem and that is suicide.

— Albert Camus
The Myth of Sisyphus

Lying on his deathbed, T is scribbling a suicide note. Although T is near his natural death, yet he feels he will die by suicide. T has been contemplating it for many years. But unable to pen down a suicide note to his liking, he could not come to the final act. It is not that T has something important to say to anyone. T also does not harbor illusions that his suicide note would be of some literary merit. He very well knows that no one would take any interest in it. Still, a suicide without a memo would be incongruous to the society he belongs to. He has spent all his life according to the prevailing social and cultural mores. All his life's major decisions have been taken under societal pressure. While departing, therefore, T does not want to break any norm.

If you can give wings to your imagination, you can envision T's entire life as a bunch of keys—each key represents a phase in his life. His society manufactured these keys and hung around his neck when he was born. These keys open different doors and have words like Religion, Education, Job, Marriage, and Kids engraved on them. There are a few blank keys as well. When T first discovered them, he tried hard to decipher the meaning behind the nothingness. T roamed around, looking for an answer. All the key makers in his society said that these were just bad jobs done by an uncaring artisan. The well-known key makers dismissed these keys as an aberration. However, the meaninglessness of these keys kept T up for many nights. It was around these nightly meditations, he decided to embrace death. It was a declaration that life may not be worth the trouble, after all. This was the first time T experienced free will within himself. But the practice of writing a suicide note before suicide restricted the rebel within him. Society has ways to work around once it is inside an individual.

T never talked about suicide with anyone. Sometimes, he would share his half-written suicide notes with people to read. A few of them would show their sentiments upon reading them. But no significant discussion ever ensued. A few months ago, he wrote about a time when his desire for suicide was least. He mentioned meeting and separating from someone. Many read it, but no one asked T as to how they were separated or why they even met? He came to realize that in his culture, it was acceptable to assemble and separate. T accepted the practice as a cultural norm where two people would come together at a certain age, and then they stay apart after a while. Like two pieces of twigs floating in a river, they approach and touch each other for a brief time and separate forever. Only a trace is left on each, creating a desire for unity. T came to believe that for relationships like these, his society created those nameless keys, especially for relationships without names. These keys were only meant to develop clinking sound in his life and add some weight to it, without which the bunch would become a collection of keys, merely a material existence, devoid of any spiritual value. T wrote about it in his last suicide note.

Of course, by performing suicide, T wants to rebel against his society. But he does not want to violate any of the social norms. At least, T does not want to dismiss those keys which open doors that lead him to rooms where he can live in the present in peace with himself. He mentioned this aspect in detail in his essay, "Existence Beyond Hope and Regret." Here's another example that reveals how much importance T gives to societal regulations. When he was debating intensely with himself, the question of suicide, he frankly talked about the need to save his society. But keeping it safe from whom— he never revealed. His friends indulged him on his face, but at his back, no one even remembered what he said. One day, his friends, perhaps overwhelmed by his monologue ad nauseam, dismissed him by saying that only beauty would save the world. T was hurt, for many called him ugly at the time of his birth. T's plan to save his society was undone at his birth. Around this time, he concluded about performing suicide. T once discussed his plans with Camus, but the matter of a suicide note was never brought up.

T's suicide note is now nearing completion. His life has traveled into its final leg of the journey— the doctors are planning to remove his life support devices. The nurses are jiggling the bunch of keys around T's neck, looking for the keys bearing his religion and the address of his cemetery. Tomorrow, T, after struggling to write a suicide note all his life, will be confined between the two dates, as a matter of bureaucratic detail. Tomorrow, a condolence meeting will happen, where the members of his society will come carrying their bunch of keys hung around their necks. In each's neck, those nameless keys will also clink, whose sound on such an occasion troubles everyone. The sound is soaked in the noise of time—the noise that is relentless and meaningless. There also exists a sweet melody of life, which remains above this noise. T must have heard this music.

LONELINESS
four tiny tales

A WORM

A worm crawls over the ceiling of my room. It has crawled here for months, leaving trails and imprints, of varied sizes and shapes, resembling its own.

When imprints were few, I had slept, through my weariness, counting them and locating the worm. Now, even on my most attentive nights, I fail to find it. But imprints now quiver more. Maybe, by memories.

The worm seemingly inhabits all of my ceilings. It seems present everywhere, yet harder to find, like the omnipresent God.

I have looked for it, in vain, for nights and days on weekends and holidays. I took pictures and videos from my cell-phone and sat through my lunch breaks and commute time, to isolate the worm from its many images. More I looked at them, more they quivered in mechanical unison from a distance, and more lifeless they were on closer examination.

Sometimes, when in my room, I feel I have found the beast. I throw my slipper on it. Yet, I fail to find its crushed corpse, pus, or mucous dripping from the roof or anything suggesting life. The slipper rebounds and falls back on me, as if the roof is hitting me again.

My head also itches in the aftermath, as if something is crawling inside.

Is it living inside me? Can it be me?

MEANINGS

In such meetings and partings lives are ultimately lost
There is no end to love, and beauty never relents
—Meer Taqi Meer
(translated by Shamsur Rahman Faruqi)

Earlier, the meanings of a few things were not so rigid. They had the flexibility of context within them. But after meeting and parting from you, certain things have hardened in their meanings.

Now, whenever I see small tea glasses, which are often used in roadside tea-shops, I remember the time I used to spend waiting for you in the tea-shop outside your college. In those tiny glasses, I used to sip time more than the tea itself. Even today, when I drink tea at a kiosk, I feel I am waiting for you.

Something similar happens when I hop on a bus. I always bought two tickets. Even today, sometimes, I buy two. One for me, and another for memories, that time has converted into bus tickets by its craft.

Often, I throw a tennis ball into my neighbor's courtyard and walk up to his door to ask for the ball, wishing that you would return to this house and open the door. Though I do this on the insistence of the tennis ball, some hope I also bear.

I don't know how many objects, memories will leave its imprints on, and how many more meanings will fade by the stain of time?

Sometimes, I see your early separation as a blessing, else how difficult it would have been for my small world to cope with so much loss in meanings.

MOST USELESS

It was the usual weekend. Time had slowed down. I was looking for things to do. I began searching for my apartment for the most useless thing there. By night, I managed to put my hands on a two-year-old movie ticket. As I was going to dispose of it, I felt a rousing voice emanating from the ticket. I heard it saying—You searched for me, turned your apartment upside down, and found me, so, you see, I am not so useless after all, you still sought me, but who comes looking for you, or asks about you.

SOLITUDE

Disenchanted, he is hiding from everyone. One day, he shuts himself in a room and decides never to come out. He has a few books with him. He reads them in various ways—left to right, bottom to top, individual pages he reads all day long, sometimes, only a few particular words time and again. He says the world, by whose form he is disturbed, from which he is running away and wants to rebuild, appears new each time he reads his books differently. In that room, he imagines his world outside. By changing the order of the books, their arrangements, he keeps changing it. The room becomes a grave for him, in whose confinement he experiences freedom.

If graves are not maintained from outside, with time, their mounds flatten. Or, if it rains, and water settles over it, the earth caves in, and quite mercilessly, exposes the inside of a grave and makes it a half-closed shallow pit. A certain proportion of light and darkness makes a partially opened grave mysterious. In our society, there are two schools of thought on the maintenance of cemeteries. Both of them offer creepy arguments in their support and never agree. How would seventy dead bodies fit inside in a grave on the day of judgment, if a burial is maintained and used only by one dead body? This is one side's most potent argument. The other side claims that a deceased person lives inside a grave, and the dwelling must be maintained. Sometimes, people discipline their kids by telling them about these half-opened graves. All these discussions also bring to life the much-forgotten dead person. People recount the deeds and calculate if the opening of the tomb is a good or bad omen. If the deceased is the right person, people say that the sacred soul has returned, moved by the injustices of the world. If the evil deeds outweigh the good, the grave is considered broken and not opened, and some natural justice has been meted out to the poor person.

The grave of his room caved in that day when a face came at his doors. The face had a tenderness, by which he thought it to be of some female. There were numerous wrinkles on her face, which he divides into different categories. The bruises were least prominent, but they had a certain redness to them, as if fresh. The wrinkles marking poverty were like rivers marked on a black-and-white geographical map, dark and bold. Despair and sadness lines were deep, but they changed their shapes frequently, expanding, and shrinking. The contours due to age are shallow, or they appear in comparison. A few wrinkles are on both sides of lips, symmetrical. Perhaps of some frozen smile. It seems that she had smiled centuries ago, but immediately something like snow must have fallen in her life that these remnants still appear shivering and frozen. He sees a story in each of her wrinkles as if not face, but he is peering at a book. Reading, he gets lost. He gives her a cold stare. Her face, out of helplessness, shrouds itself in a smile. He could see in her smile his cold reflection. Embarrassed, he immediately looks down.

He again looks up at her. Her eyes appeared to him like two lakes, deep and calm. Below those eyes, he also notices a green algal layer. He stretches his hand to wipe off the green slime, but he fails. The cascade begins to flow out of her eyes. The tears after getting out of her eyes, touch her face, and immediately split into many streams, flowing along with the wrinkles. These streams gently collect in a common point near her chins and begin falling on his doors. The water started accumulating on his grave. The weight of water, becoming too much for the earth to bear, opens the grave. He begins preparing for his return. According to worldly wisdom, this is like a life-death cycle, but to him, it appears as a life-life cycle. He thinks if his solitude does not lead him back to society, it will become a spiritual dead end, a real grave. He steps out of his room and wipes the tears from her face.

A Prologue to Lynching

An evening prayer assembly was going on in the village. Jeduji, the head priest, was narrating the story of the goddess Stega, who had taken the human form of a stegosaurus to protect her people. The villagers worshipped stegosaurus as Mother goddess and called it *Mathra.*

It was the worst of famines, continued Jeduji. Even the weeds refused to grow here. First, the birds left the village, followed by cats, dogs, and cattle. The trees also seemed to attempt fleeing—uprooting themselves and falling. Those living 'out there'— Jeduji pointed finger to his back, learned to eat the fleeing animals. The villagers understood the gesture, for they all referred to the village of flesh-eaters as 'out there.' We ate the roots of the trees that fell, considering them as food from our ancestors. We were the farmers' community, and our ancestors maintained this crucial practice of eating from the soil and vegetation. But those who lived 'out there' became a hunting community, always surviving on flesh. The assembly was listening to Jeduji's discourse in rapt attention.

The ancestors then organized a ritual, and then *Mathra* appeared as a stegosaurus at the edge of our village. At first, no one could understand the miracle and feared her appearance. But wherever *Mathra* sat, grass grew, her dung sprouted a green forest, and her urine forged rivers. Prosperity had returned with *Mathra's* grace. The villagers went ecstatic by this end of the story, and *Jamat* members chanted slogans in praise of *Mathra*. Some had brought fruits with them and started offering to stegosauruses roaming around.

Jeduji continued—but those who lived 'out there' ate the flesh of our *Mathra*, staying with their barbaric ways of their hunter ancestors. These *mallechas* even today eat *Mathra*, though they too claim her as divine but as a father figure. They worship her as *Pithra* and have temples in his honor, but what blasphemy is this that they eat off their god's flesh, that too when She is our Mother goddess? She is our *Mathra*. Can you believe this nonsense?

Sensing his listeners becoming a little tensed by now, Jeduji brought another aspect into the discourse. You know what, we, the farming community, respect women and include them in our work, but have you heard of any *mallecha* woman participating in any hunt? They just want to dominate their women, keeping them within their homes. The women villagers seemed to agree and considered themselves grateful to their men in the village. Gaea sitting in the discourse with her toddler child, Bhoonsa, in her lap, kept an eye on her house, waiting for her husband, Neru, to return. She noticed a shadow that looked unlike Neru entering her home. Gaea, tucking Bhoonsa in her armpit, rushed toward the shadow.

Now in *saneema,* no one plays the role of a farmer—rued Neru.

The crops failing each year and income gone, Neru, a farmer, found no glamor in his hardships. He often remembered his good old days, the little of which survived now, mostly in his demeanor and gait—these traits he acquired while following a famous movie star who always played brash characters. The lack of income has revealed Neru's existence to him. He saw no sense in leading a phony life. With such thoughts, Neru reached home.

Gaea had seen Neru as a shadow entering the house. Mistaking him to an intruder, she furtively approached Neru holding a stick in an attacking way. Neru turned, and she froze for a while.

"You scared me." These words brought Gaea to her usual self. But, they failed to incite any response in Neru. The words seemed to voicelessly drown in Neru's deep-set eyes as if they were uttered hours ago. Gaea spoke again to break the silence.

"Why do you walk so differently today?"

"This is how I walk. What's wrong with it?"—Neru took half-asleep Bhoonsa from Gaea.

"Where have you been, watching *saneema* at Nonua's?"

Neru looked the other way.

"Jeduji was looking for you before the discourse."—Neru stretched on the bed, putting Bhoonsa next to him. Both drew close to each other. Gaea continued speaking. It lulled Neru to sleep. Soon silence swept the house. Occasionally, their old, rickety bed groaned, but that was it. Even that sound had silence interspersed within it as if silence was an actual being who guarded the house and leaped on any music and muted it after some scuffle.

Neru's dream adulterated his sleep. He saw a massive crowd at his doorstep, and then a stegosaurus appeared. When he woke up, he remembered only the stegosaurus. The image remained with him all day long. He confided this to Gaea. She considered it a divine message.

"We are going to Jeduji."—Gaea moved at once, Neru remained passive.

"He often asks of you."—Gaea's voice had a subtle prayer to it. Neru, like the god to the prayers, was unmoved. Exasperated, Gaea tucked Bhoonsa under her armpit and left. Neru, finding nothing else to do, followed her to the temple.

The place where Neru lived was hard to say if it was a village or a city. Time refused to grow there; to make up for the loss, it had put objects belonging to the prevalent taste here and there. The contradictions were so plentiful that one would first not believe them, and think of this place as some museum, perhaps of time itself. But the poetry went as far, on a closer look, the area cried its tragedy. A mobile tower stood casting its slant shadow on the thatched huts whose occupants, after eating their meals, often worried for the next ones. Sitting under the same shadow, some fret over their mobile data. A pucca road pierced the muddy terrains all around it, and *development* came as much close.

Crossing this road barefooted, they reached the temple, where the evening prayer session had just concluded. The temple gate would now be closed, and *Mathra* would retire for Her nightly rest. Gaea rushed to take the last glimpse of *Mathra* seated there, failing, which would make her night miserable with guilt. She did not want to lose her sleep to visit the temple and not able to have a glimpse of *Mathra*. Seeing her coming with Neru, Jeduji delayed closing the gate. After completing her prayer, Gaea approached Jeduji, who, sitting on the stairs, pretended some occupation with his mobile phone.

"He dreamed of a stegosaurus last night."— Gaea told Jeduji.

Jeduji held Neru in his eyes for a while and then looked away. Neru looked at Jeduji without much interest. After Gaea stopped speaking, Jeduji stood up and walked to the end of the stairs and signaled Neru to follow him. Both, as if by some secret understanding, conversed only in gestures. Jeduji took Neru to the backside of the temple. Three more men soon approached them. One of them began speaking, "We are from *Jamat*, we rescue stegosauruses, we need people like you to protect our *Mathra*. Neru, after listening patiently, began walking back toward Gaea, whom Jeduji already gestured to go back. Neru had been seeing her back, reducing to a point in space. She occasionally turned around to see what was going on. But visible only as a silhouette, it was hard for Neru to tell when she faced him and when her back. He withstood the conversation by staring at her, vanishing into the horizon. "*Ekhajar* for every stegosaurus rescued." Neru's retreating steps halted, only to turn and walk back to the three men. The deal closed at eighteen hundred. Jeduji, disgusted with what the world has come to, simply walked away. Neru, too, walked back to his house.

It was getting dark. Even darker were thoughts settling in Neru's heart. He thought about his dwindling income and the family's needs. The idea made the darkness around him continuous, his inner world indistinguishable from the impending black night as if he exhaled night from his nostrils—a black smoke merging everything with their shadows. Engulfed in this darkness as if his ears had a vision, he saw a stegosaurus moo. A man emerged from his silhouette, flogging the stegosaurus. The sight caused no pity or devotion in him. Instead, he was overcome by greed and feeling of power. He ran to the man and slapped him.

"Is this your stegosaurus? Tell your name…"— only these words, repeatedly told between expletives, made sense, for many others just drowned in saliva and its froth forming at the edge of Neru's mouth.

"This-is-not-mine-it-belongs-to-*maalik*-I-only-work-for-him." The words, all at once, fell from his mouth as if he had forever stacked them there, only to say them now.

"Boss?"

"Samir Seth!"

"Samir Seth!" The name excited Neru, sensing an opportunity, his fury multiplied, though deep within he felt elated.

"Tell your *maalik* to collect the stegosaurus from *Jamat* tomorrow." Neru snapped the leash from the man's hand and took the stegosaurus away. He began walking toward his house. The night no longer seemed dark, the sky and its stars sparkled, like Neru's eyes.

Reaching home, Neru tied the stegosaurus in the courtyard and immediately rushed to the backyard picking up a *lota* to relieve himself, without caring to look at Bhoonsa, who was playing with eggplants in the yard. Gaea was cooking meals in the kitchen. The child held the eggplant in his hand toward the stegosaurus, as a gesture of offering food. The stegosaurus opened its mouth and devoured the eggplant. Delighted Bhoonsa offered more. While in the kitchen, the *chulha* growled as Gaea lit it up with matches. Neru returned from the backyard and bolted the door. A scream suddenly rose from Bhoonsa's mouth. Neru saw the kid dangling with his hand in the jaws of the stegosaurus. He immediately threw his *lota*, hitting it. Neru went after the stegosaurus with everything around—sticks, bricks, fists, kicks. Bhoonsa fell from its mouth. Gaea rushed and took Bhoonsa in her lap and began beating her chest. Lying on the ground, the stegosaurus breathed with a whimpering sound. By then, a crowd had gathered outside Neru's house. He was too exhausted to check on the people gathered at his door, knocking. The blood was spattered on the ground. The stegosaurus had become still. The crowd at the door barged in when they failed to get any response from inside. Samir Seth, himself a *Jamat* member, had come to take his stegosaurus back. Neru saw the rush of frantic human feet flowing in his courtyard and drowning him in. His eyes blinked and finally closed.